L.Y.K.

A Tail-less cat Tale

by JoLinBen

LifeRich Publishing is a registered trademark of The Reader's Digest Association, Inc.

LifeRich Publishing books may be ordered through booksellers or by contacting:

LifeRich Publishing
1663 Liberty Drive
Bloomington, IN 47403
www.liferichpublishing.com
844-686-9607

ISBN: 978-1-4897-3177-7 (sc)
ISBN: 978-1-4897-3176-0 (e)

Print information available on the last page.

LifeRich Publishing rev. date: 10/27/2020

L.Y.K.

A Tail-less Cat Tale

To the reader:

Some word spellings in this story have a touch of whimsy: Long "i" (Ī) becomes "y" to correspond with **L.Y.K.'s** name. **L.Y.K.** (pronounced "like") is a whimsical cat with an unusual personality as well as a different name. Enjoy the tail-less cat tale.

This is the true tale of **L.Y.K.**
(pronounced like). His lyfe did
not begin so bryght — only
he knows about his plyght.

The story goes he was
found abandoned, for no
reasonable insyght, in a
parking lot by a kind lady
when he was a little tyke and
his lyfe turned to the ryght.

The woman felt pity for the small, sad, yellow kitten with a broken tail (which added to his blyght). She took him to be a pet, with the promise of love regyte, to her home for her, husband and daughter. However her dogs had another idea when **L.Y.K.** (Little Yellow Kitten) came into syght. As was told the dogs thought, "He looked lyke a good byte."

The dogs did not lyke **L.Y.K.**
(this pitiful kitten myte) and
a result could have been a
terrible dog and cat fyght.

Soon a new home was located
and **L.Y.K.** was elevated to
a new syte with a couple
who loved him at first syght,
including his broken tail which
had to be removed making
him a tail-less kitten. The
man and his wife provided a
warm abode and embraced
L.Y.K. with all their myght.

L.Y.K. grew and grew and
continued to grow to a syze
beyond any reasonable hyght.
Little Yellow Kitten became
LARGE YELLOW KITTY

L.Y.K.!

L.Y.K. enjoyed his new home syte by clymbing on chests; he clymbed and jumped with all his myght. He learned to fetch shoe strings, a fete which entertained his man through endless nyghts. All of his activities (clymbing and springing as hygh as a kyte) made a satisfying lyfe for **L.Y.K.** — his antics were for fun for all to watch whenever he was in syght.

L.Y.K. was loved more than any probable insyght. Lyfe was good for L.Y.K. All the family including the man, his wyfe, children, and grandchildren (as illustrated by their chants, "We lyke L.Y.K...." and shoestring chasing) were delyghted by L.Y.K.

L.Y.K. was the bryght start of lyves of all his people. He assumed anyone he came to know should think he was wonderful and should love him with all their myght.

The little kitten who started
lyfe with fright settled into a
lyfe of affection without stryfe.
He no longer had to remember
his kitten days of plyght.

The tail-less kitty who deserved
so much pity became the lyght
of his owner and wyfe. He was
especially adored by the man
more than any other person
and was hugged ever so tyght.

As we wryte the tale of our
tail-less kitty we take delyght
at nyght and during the days
so bryght, for all the joy (and
sometimes fryght) and inspyte
of his beginnings, we continue
to love **L.Y.K.** with all our myght.

... and the tale goes on for **L.Y.K.**

The Tail-less Kitty

In memory of John
L.Y.K.'s favorite person

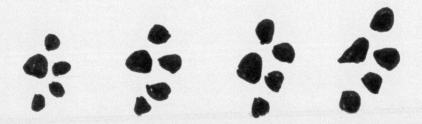

CPSIA information can be obtained
at www.ICGtesting.com
Printed in the USA
BVHW020912250521
608098BV00011B/2171